ISBN 1 85854 742 3
Published by Brimax Books Ltd, Newmarket, England, CB8 7AU 1998.
Printed in Spain.

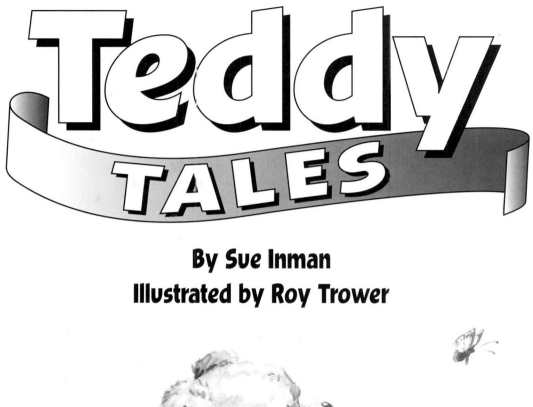

Teddy TALES

By Sue Inman
Illustrated by Roy Trower

Brimax · Newmarket · England

Teddy and the Ghost

Teddy and the Ghost

Teddy was bored.
"I know," said Teddy. "I'll make
some mud castles in the garden."
Teddy made four mud castles.
Then he built a wall joining them
all together. He dug a moat and
then he poured water into it.
Teddy collected lots of pebbles
and stuck them to the castle walls.

Teddy was very pleased with himself. Then just as he turned to go inside, he saw it. A ghost! It was big and white and drifting across the grass. Teddy could see two dark patches that looked like eyes! Teddy was scared.

"AAAGH!" cried Teddy as he ran into the house. "Dad! Dad!" he yelled.

Father Bear was nowhere to be found. Teddy ran back into the kitchen. Through the window he saw something strange. Father Bear was running around the garden. Teddy forgot how frightened he was and peeped around the kitchen door. Father Bear was chasing the ghost! Round the garden he ran, trying to catch it. But every time he came close to it, the ghost drifted off.

Just then Father Bear saw Teddy.
"Help me, Teddy!" he yelled. "The
wind is blowing the sheets away
and they're getting muddy!"
The ghost was really a sheet!
That evening when Teddy went to
bed he was still giggling. But in the
night he was woken by a strange
sound: "Woooo! Woooo!"
"It's only the wind," said Teddy.
But he was never really sure...

Teddy Falls in Love

A new family of bears had moved next door to Teddy. Mirabelle Bear was the same age as Teddy. Teddy liked Mirabelle straight away. Soon Teddy found himself thinking about her all the time.

"I must love Mirabelle," said Teddy to Mother Bear one day. "If I love her, I should marry her."

"You're too young to get married," said Mother Bear.

"I'll wait until I'm old enough," said Teddy. "I'll send her a Valentine's Day card and ask her to wait, too." Teddy began making his card. He drew hearts and flowers and painted them brightly. When the card was finished, Teddy wrote a message inside. It said: 'Dear Mirabelle, I would like to marry you when I'm old enough, so please wait. Love from T'.

On Valentine's Day, Teddy got up early to deliver his card. He took an orange to eat on the way. As Teddy walked along, he saw Mirabelle! Mirabelle smiled. Teddy grinned back. As he did, the juice from his orange squirted out of his mouth and dribbled down his chin! Mirabelle laughed. Teddy felt very silly. He ran all the way home.

Teddy hid in his bedroom. He would have stayed there all day but Father Bear called him downstairs. A card had been delivered for him. Teddy opened it. A huge smile spread across his face. On the front of the card were hearts and flowers, and the words inside said: 'Dear Teddy, I would like to marry you when I'm old enough, so please wait. Love from M'.

Can you find five differences between these two pictures?

What is Teddy doing?

digging

drawing

running

smiling

Teddy and the Beanstalk

Teddy and the Beanstalk

It was lunchtime. Teddy looked at his plate. "Where do beans come from?" he asked Mother Bear. "They grow," said Mother Bear. "How do they grow?" asked Teddy. "I'll show you," said Mother Bear. She filled a plant pot with soil. Then she planted a bean. She watered the pot and put it in a sunny spot in the garden.

"A beanstalk will grow. The beans come from the beanstalk," said Mother Bear.

"What if I want an orange?" asked Teddy.

"Then you must plant an orange seed," said Mother Bear.

"What I plant is what will grow!" said Teddy. He filled a pot with soil. Then Teddy took something from his pocket and planted it in the soil. He watered the pot and put it in the sun.

The following week Teddy and Mother Bear looked in their pots. In Mother Bear's pot, they saw a small, green shoot. But in Teddy's pot, they saw a large, pink shoot!

"What did you plant in your pot, Teddy?" gasped Mother Bear.

"A jellybean!" said Teddy with a grin.

"You are silly!" laughed Mother Bear.

Teddy and the Play

Teddy heard the door bell ring. Mouse, Squirrel and Rabbit were standing on the doorstep.

"Hello, Teddy," said Mouse. "It's my Dad's birthday on Sunday and we're going to put on a play for him in the school hall. Will you be in it?"

"Oh, yes please!" said Teddy. He hoped he might be given the most important part in the play. After all, he was the biggest.

"We want you to be a tree," said Mouse.

"A tree?" said Teddy in surprise.

"Yes, Rabbit will hide behind you," said Mouse.

Teddy decided to be the best tree ever seen in a play. He put on his brown jeans to look like a tree trunk, and his green sweatshirt to look like leaves. He stood with his arms in the air like branches.

By Sunday Teddy had a cold. It was too late to find someone else to be the tree. Mouse and Squirrel stuck leaves and twigs to Teddy to make him look like a real tree. Now all the grown-ups were arriving at the hall. Teddy went to his place on the stage and became a tree. Teddy's friends started to act out the play. They were just getting to the most exciting part when the 'tree' felt a tickle in his nose. "AAAATISHOO!" sneezed the tree.

It was such a big sneeze that poor Rabbit was knocked off his feet. He picked himself up and brushed leaves and twigs from his head. He started to say his next line but no one heard it.

"AAAATISHOO!" sneezed the tree again. Teddy felt miserable. He was ruining the play and Mouse would be sad.

The friends carried on, but they had to shout their lines! When the play was finished, Father Mouse wiped tears of laughter from his eyes. "That was the best birthday present I've ever had," he said. "The play was very good. I liked the sneezing tree. Whose idea was that?"

Can you find five differences between these two pictures?

What is Teddy doing?

eating

planting

smiling

sneezing

Teddy's Lost Toy

Teddy's Lost Toy

Teddy was glad to be going to Grandma's house for the day. Mother Bear was spring-cleaning. Teddy was bored. He sat on the doorstep waiting for Grandma to arrive. Suddenly there was a shout from upstairs.

"Teddy! Come quickly!" cried Mother Bear.

Teddy went upstairs to his bedroom. "Look what I've found!" said Mother Bear, holding up a small, dusty, cuddly toy that didn't look like anything at all. "It's Thing!" "THING!" cried Teddy joyfully. "You've been found at last!" And he hugged the long lost toy and danced around the room with it. "Oh, Thing!" said Teddy. "I promise never to lose you again..." He was interrupted by Grandma knocking at the door.

Teddy put his toy on his pillow.
Because he was sad to leave it
behind, he picked it up again. He
put it down and then picked it up,
put it down and then picked it up
until Mother Bear told him to hurry.
Teddy ran downstairs. Grandma
helped him into her car and they
drove off. Teddy loved visiting
Grandma and they had a big lunch
at her house followed by ice cream
for dessert. Then they went to the
park to play and stopped for
hotdogs on the way home.

When they arrived home, Teddy saw that something was wrong.
The house was a terrible mess.
Teddy's friends were there too.
They seemed to be looking for something.
"What's going on?" Teddy asked Mother Bear.
"Poor Teddy," she said. "I don't know how to tell you this... Thing is lost again."
Teddy gulped.
"I noticed he was missing after you left. I must have put him somewhere..." said Mother Bear.

"We've looked everywhere," said Teddy's friend Squirrel.

"Even in the garden," said Rabbit. Everyone tried to cheer up Teddy. At last Teddy said, "I think this is my fault, you see..." And with that Teddy pulled something small and dusty from his pocket.

"THING!" cried Mother Bear. Everyone started chasing Teddy across the garden. When they caught him, they tickled him until he begged them to stop.

Teddy and the Sea Monster

Waves lapped around Teddy's ankles. The sun was warm on his back. A big smile crept across his face as he gazed out at the sea. "This is the life," he said to himself. Teddy turned to wave to his family, watching him from the beach. Then he turned back to the sea again. And he screamed loudly.

"AAAGH!" cried Teddy, running up the beach as fast as he could.

"What's wrong?" asked Mother Bear.

"A monster in the sea!" gasped Teddy, out of breath.

"A monster?" said Mother Bear.

"Yes! It was HORRIBLE! It had a big, black nose with a hook like an umbrella handle - that's all I could see above the water," said poor Teddy.

"Perhaps I should take a look," said Mother Bear.

"I'll come too," said Grandma, who had been around long enough to see most kinds of monsters.

They walked to the water's edge. Suddenly the monster reared up out of the sea. It *was* horrible! There was the black nose with a hook like an umbrella handle that Teddy had seen. Now he could see its big, glassy eyes, enormous, furry body and webbed feet. It was too scary. Teddy hid his eyes. But Grandma and Mother Bear were laughing. Teddy decided to look with one eye. He did feel silly. The monster was grinning at him. It said, "Hello, Teddy."

"Hello, Dad," said Teddy!

Can you find five differences between these two pictures?

What are they doing?

cleaning

tickling

waving

pointing

Teddy's Shadow

Teddy's Shadow

It was a sunny day. Teddy was
walking through the meadow.
The sun went behind a cloud.
Teddy saw that his shadow was
gone. After a while he met Rabbit
who was fishing by the lake.
"Have you seen my shadow?"
Teddy asked. "I've lost it!"
"No, Teddy, but I think..." began
Rabbit.

But Teddy ran off, searching for his shadow. Then Teddy passed Squirrel in his garden.
"Have you seen my shadow?" Teddy asked Squirrel. "I've lost it!"
"No I haven't, Teddy, but I think..." began Squirrel.
But Teddy was in too much of a hurry. He ran off, searching for his shadow.

Next Teddy met Mouse who was
feeding the ducks.
"Have you seen my shadow?"
Teddy asked Mouse. "I've lost it!"
"No I haven't, Teddy, but I think..."
began Mouse.
But Teddy was in too much of a
hurry. He ran off, searching for his
shadow.

Teddy was still searching for his shadow when the sun came out from behind the cloud. Then he noticed his shadow was on the ground again. Just then Rabbit, Squirrel and Mouse caught up with Teddy. Now they could finish telling him what they thought...

"...You'll find your shadow when the sun comes out!" they all said together.

Who will Play with Teddy?

On Teddy's birthday, his Grandma gave him a new kite. When Teddy woke up the next day to find the sun shining, he went to Squirrel's house and knocked on the door. When Squirrel opened the door, Teddy said, "Would you like to come and play with my new kite?" But Squirrel took one look at Teddy, screamed loudly and slammed the door.

So Teddy went to call on Rabbit. But when Rabbit saw Teddy, he screamed loudly and slammed the door, too.

"What is wrong with everyone today?" said Teddy. He decided to try Mouse. He knocked on the door. "Mouse, would you like..." Teddy started to say. But Mouse took one look at Teddy, screamed loudly, and slammed the door.

Teddy began to cry. He walked home all alone.

When Mother Bear saw Teddy coming up the path, she threw her arms in the air.

"Oh, you poor little bear!" she cried.

Then she whisked Teddy off to bed.

"What's going on?" asked Teddy.

But before Mother Bear could answer, there was a knock at the door.

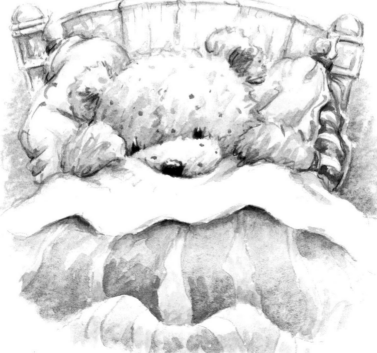

Teddy could hear his friends talking to Mother Bear downstairs.

"Have you seen it?" asked Squirrel.

"It's horrible!" said Rabbit.

"A big, spotty monster!" said Mouse.

"You silly animals!" said Mother Bear. "You haven't seen a monster! That was Teddy. He has the measles."

Rabbit, Squirrel and Mouse thought Teddy was a monster because he was covered in spots. They didn't mean to be unfriendly. Teddy felt much better all ready!

Can you find five differences between these two pictures?

What are they doing?

searching

fishing

knocking

crying

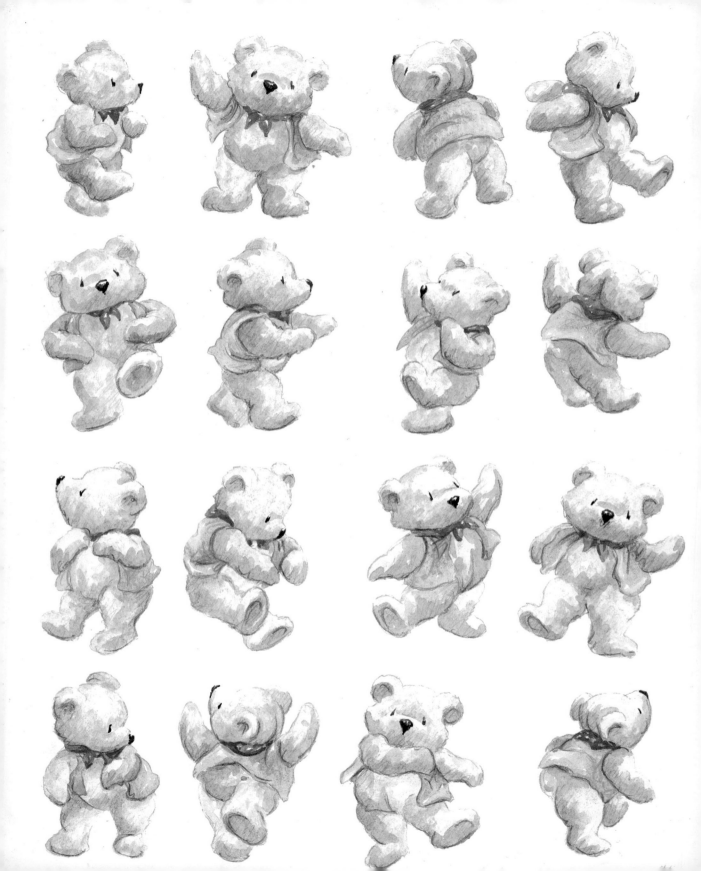